Being Candy - An LGBT, First Time, Feminization, New Adult, Short-Read Romance

by Barbara Deloto and Thomas Newgen

Other books written by Barb and Tom
Shapeshifter
Changes
Changes II
Virgin Bride
Virgin Call Girl
My Wife's Success
Bored Guys
Hypnotized
*An Addicted Cross-Dresser, Married, and a Happy Ending - A True Story: A
Book to Share*
Feminizing Men - A Guide to Maximize the Feminization of a Male
Feminizing Men - A Tale of a Husband's Forced Feminization by His Hot Wife
*My Hot Wife - A Cuckold, Male Chastity, Female Led Relationship, Feminization
Story*
Rose's Bud Becomes a Blossom
Male Chastity and Crossdressing as Tools for the Cuckolding Hot Wife
*Forced Feminization: A Hot Wife, Cuckold, Forced Fem, Male Chastity,
Feminized Men, Shemale Slut Story*
Crossdressing- A College Boy is Feminized
Crossdressing - A Stepbrother is Feminized
*Realizing Jessica - A Femboy Gets Fem and Discovers Inner Passions and
Love*
Desires- Fantasy Becomes Reality for an Occasional Crossdresser
Trannies - Two Guys Get Fem
Jessica's Turn: A Gender-Bending LGBT Romance
Frat House - A Gender-Bending LGBT Romance
*Finishing School - A Boy Is Sent to a Girls' Finishing School - An LGBT
Romance*
All Dolled Up: A Student Gets Fem - An LGBT Romance
Sissy Boyfriend

1

I woke with a start and sat bolt upright in bed. "What happened?" I looked around the room. "Why am I here?"

A nurse came in; I stared at her. "Ah, wonderful. She's awake now." She came over to me and took my pulse. "Are you feeling well, Candy?"

"Candy? My name isn't Candy—it's Robert. Hey, what happened to my voice?"

"I guess you could still go by Robert if you'd like, but...well, your identity has been changed as well as your voice, and your outward appearance certainly isn't a Robert—just as you wished." She smiled at me.

I thought, *Candy. What a stupid name.* I asked, "And my voice I sounds like a bimbo. Why?"

The nurse giggled. "It is a bit ditsy-sounding, but cute. Sometimes they scrape the vocal cords a little more than they should, just to be sure, but the good news is that no one will ever think it's a man's voice. It matches your look perfectly, for being a girl called Candy. Why are you so shocked? Did you forget you had feminization surgeries?"

My wife said, "She's just disoriented yet. She'll be okay."

The nurse nodded. "Yes, of course, Dr. Mitchell. You should know."

Gender surgeries? I panicked and felt under the sheets. I still had it, thank god.

I looked at my wife. "What the hell, Joey?"

Smiling down at me, she put her hand on my head. "It's your dream come true, like she said, sweetie. I know it's overwhelming, having all the changes at once, but I thought it would be easier for you from a physical standpoint, not having to go into the hospital over and over for multiple anesthesia and surgeries. This is how you were meant to be. You'll get used to being Candy."

I felt my new breasts under the hospital gown. They were breasts, all right. Hard, sensitive nipples and all. Sore, but breasts. I leapt from the bed and had to steady myself at first, since my body felt out of balance. I think the breasts were tugging me forward with their weight. I carefully walked over to the bathroom and looked in the mirror.

My cheeks were higher and plump, my lips thick and luscious and colored a bimbo pink, and my eyes had eyeliner on them. I tried to wash it off in the sink.

My wife came in. "If you're trying to wash off your lipstick and eyeliner, they're permanent. Thought we might as well have that done while you were out."

I stood, wiped my face with a towel and looked into the mirror. My hair had been cut in layers in a woman's style and colored with streaks of auburn and blond. My ears had stud earrings in them in three places. I stared at my reflection. "What the hell did you do to me, Joey!?"

She slapped my bottom. "Nice ass, baby."

"Ow!" I slid my hands over it feeling the size of it. I had hips and large, firm butt cheeks.

I lifted the hospital gown and looked at my body. "Oh my god. I have the body of a woman."

"Very much the body of a woman. Most women would die for a body like yours. Except, of course, you have something they don't have, with your last remaining vestige of maleness between your legs. We can always chop it off, if it feels out of place to you, and make a proper receptacle there."

"No way!" I ran my hands over my face and body, looking in the mirror. "All my body hair is gone too."

"Of course, dear. You didn't have much anyway. I thought it would be good to have electrolysis done while you were out to make you smooth and silky. And you'll never need to shave your legs, face, chest, or pubic area now. Now be a good girl and brush your teeth, shower, and dry your hair, then dress and we'll go."

The nurse said, "You look lovely, Candy. You're the best male-to-female transformation I've ever seen. I think you were meant for this, and I can see why you wanted to do it. You must be very happy."

"I, uh, I..."

Joey said, "Quiet, dear. I know it's better than you imagined, and it must be shocking how well it came out."

The nurse looked at my wife. "Dr. Mitchell, you must be proud and happy that your husband has finally become the she he always felt he should be. So, I did I hear Candy say she won't be doing the last surgery yet? If so, I won't schedule it for her."

My wife looked at me and shook her head. She looked at the nurse. "Not right now. Maybe someday if she wants it, since it might mess the lines of her clothing, and maybe she'll be annoyed by it."

"Very good then. I'll leave you two to get Candy ready." She left the room and closed the door.

Joey looked at me. "What do you think, Candy? Do you want to get rid of your old candy?" She laughed.

My eyes popped open. "Don't even think about it. Stop talking about it like it's some useless appendage that's marring my look."

I went to the closet. My old clothes were gone. I took the floral mini dress out and held it out to look at it.

"See the pretty things you'll get to wear now, dear?"

I glared at her and took the clothes and shoes into the bathroom.

I showered, feeling the caress of the water on my breasts, the silkiness of my skin. The more I felt my own body, the more aroused I became, because I still had my male attraction to women, and now I was one. I dried my hair, looking in the mirror. I looked like a gorgeous, sexy, bimbo of a woman.

What the hell was she thinking? How could she think I wanted this? Why was she doing this? My wife used her power as a psychiatrist to have me transformed into this, and I didn't even get a say.

I stared in the mirror, my jaw hanging. I looked at my dress, tented by a raging hard-on as my own image aroused me. I slid the panties up, and they held it tight against my belly so it couldn't be seen under the dress. I slid on the suntan thigh-high stockings, feeling them caress my legs, and slid on my high heels.

I looked in the mirror again. My large, firm, braless breasts created luscious cleavage, and my nipples made bumps in the thin fabric. I looked so provocative, every guy who saw me would want to take me, and every woman would hate me. What the hell would I do now?

How could I work in construction anymore? What in the world would I do all day?

My wife opened the door. "What's taking you so long? Come on, dear, we need to buy you clothes and get you into your new role."

"New role? What new role?"

"Well, you certainly can't be doing construction looking the way you do. The rest of the crew would have accidents, you're so distracting. I have a new purpose for you. Think of it as recycling a useless object into a useful one. Recycling useless objects is very popular these days."

"A useless object into a useful one? I was useful before."

"That's your opinion. Now at least you can make *someone* happy. You'll be very popular with the men by being candy for them. I bet you'll find a very special man to love, and make love to you."

"I am a man!"

She laughed. "You never were, and now you're what you were meant to be. You'll see—you'll love it, honey. It's who you are inside. Trust me."

2

I was beside myself with confusion, fear, and sensuality. I crossed my legs as my wife drove us. The feeling of my silky stockings slipping over each other was delicious. My breasts bounced as we ran over a bump. My long-nailed hands couldn't resist caressing my thigh.

Joey glanced at me, then turned back to the road. "See how sensual your new body is? You'll love using it."

I glared at her. "Joey, I'm only twenty-two. How could you do this to me? I mean, we got married, you finished your internship as a psychiatrist, and poof, now I'm this?"

"Of course. Why not make use of my degree to help you be your best?"

"Honey, this isn't my best. You never even *asked* me."

"It *is* your best. When I married you, I knew that I'd do this. It only made sense to. A little guy like you, you were pretty useless in construction, and not much of a man in bed either. Besides, I never wanted to be stuck with one guy all the time, and you don't need to work because I make plenty."

"Why did you even marry me then?"

"I thought it would be fun to have a girlfriend married to me who could share things. Like shopping, girl things, and men."

"Then why not marry a woman?"

"Hmm, maybe I should have. But I knew you'd be sexier and better looking than all of them after surgery. Plus, you won't be as catty or bitchy. You're nice and gentle, and I never knew a *hornier* man in my life. It seemed fitting for a horny man like you to become the object of his desire. All those times I let you have release with me… while you did nothing for me with that thing, and how quickly you'd always come! I bet you're hard as a rock right now."

"Well hell, yeah. I have the body of a hot woman. What guy wouldn't get hard? This is ridiculous. Now I'm a freak."

"A very cute and sexy freak who will be the object of desire for every man."

"But I'm not a woman. When they find out what's under my skirt, they'll beat me to death."

"Oh no, honey. They'll love it because you'll never have a period, will always look hot, and will be always horny and ready for playtime with a man.

"No way. I am *not* gay, and I won't do any of that."

"Of course you aren't gay, honey. You're a girl now, and some girls named Candy who look like you really love to please men. It's very natural. Now calm down, relax, and enjoy that gorgeous body of yours."

3

We shopped and shopped and shopped. I couldn't buy pants or tight skirts or dresses with the stuff I still had down there, but women have so many clothing options, it's astounding. My wife kept leaning toward the more revealing and sexier styles for me, and I did look incredible in them.

I loved all the shoes, jewelry, and makeup choices. Loved the feeling on my body of stockings, panties, and lingerie. Loved the perfumes we found.

All of it was a mind-blowing experience—shopping wasn't boring anymore! I must have had an effect on my wife, as well, since she bought clothes she never would have worn before. Sexy things. It was great seeing her try them on and how hot she looked in them. At least I had a hot wife to look at too.

The only problem was that I had a hard-on all day from looking at myself and my wife and trying on all the new clothes. I couldn't wait to get home and get the monkey off my back. If I even lasted that long. I might even do it in the car. Yeah, that's what I'd do. I had to just to feel *somewhat* normal again.

We made three trips to the car, dragging all our purchases, and we filled the trunk and back seat with all of it. When I was finally able to sit on the leather seat and rest, I felt better. No less horny, but better.

Joey glanced over at me. "See, wasn't that fun, honey?"

"I guess. It is more interesting and there are more options than men's shopping. I love the new dresses you bought too. I can't wait to see you in them."

"Thanks. I was watching you, and I realized I now have to look as good as you, or I won't get any guys, and you'll have them all."

"No way. I'm still your husband, and you're talking about cheating on me?"

"You don't look like my husband, and women have needs. You'll see. You'll develop new needs, too, and you'll want what a woman wants. You'll understand." She drove off.

I was so freaking horny right then. As I pictured Joey with a hunk of a guy, even though I felt jealous, it was erotic at the same time. My brain wasn't working right. I needed relief.

I slid a hand into my dress, squeezed my breast and pinched a nipple. It felt great. I slid my panties to the side and wrapped my rigid pole in the silky dress and started to beat the monkey away.

"Hey!" Joey yelled at me. She slapped the hand that was doing the jerking. "Stop that shit. You can't come yet, or I'll make sure you don't for a very long time if you do."

I glared at her. "Screw you." I jerked it some more and fondled my great tits. It felt awesome. It didn't take long before I soaked my dress with several huge loads. "Uh, god! Finally." I slumped in the seat.

Joey said, "You're gonna be so sorry you did that, you horny thing. Wait until we get home."

"You sound like my mom or something."

"Well, it seems I have to treat you like a horny little pubescent girl who can't stop masturbating."

"I had to. You did this to me. I can't be me and not be aroused now—these gorgeous tits bouncing on my chest, this fabulous, sexy body always in my sight. The feel of these clothes on me and walking in these high heels like a hooker. It's too much."

"Maybe we should chop it off."

"Joey! Stop. Why are you being so mean to me? I thought you wanted me to be your girlfriend."

"I do. I want you to be my best friend and girlfriend."

"Then treat me like one. Would you be so mean to your girlfriend?"

She thought for a moment, glanced at me, and gave me a flat smile. "You're right, honey. I have been mean. What if I help you become my girlfriend? You know. Two girls who like having fun and sharing things."

"That sounds nice. Sharing our clothes, our thoughts, our aspirations, drinks, dinner, bed. Yeah... I'd love that."

"You left a very important thing off the list."

I thought for a moment. "Hmm, makeup? You're not supposed to share makeup."

"No sweetie. *Men*. Gorgeous, real men."

"What!? C'mon, Joey, you know I have no interest in men. I'm not gay."

"Nope, you aren't. You're a girl. You're my girlfriend, and girlfriends like men. You will. Don't worry." She patted my thigh. "And the boys will love being around—and in—you. You'll have so many protein drinks and deposits made in and on you, you'll think you were on a sport diet." She laughed.

I stared out the window. She really meant what she was saying. Now I'd have to not only see my wife with other men but be a toy for them and others. I felt nauseous.

4

We reached the house, dragged all our purchases in and put them away. My old clothes were all gone, and there wasn't a single piece of male clothing or accoutrement around. Joey had evidently seen to that when I was at the hospital.

She came into the bedroom and smiled at me. "Now that you're a girl, you have to use the attachment I use on the shower. Before you get dressed, poop, shower, and use the attachment to clean out your bottom. Do it every day when you do your morning routine."

"Really? Girls do that?"

"I do. It makes one nice and fresh and clean. Go do it now."

I did, and it wasn't so bad. It did make me feel fresh and clean and was actually a little erotic. I wanted to just come in the shower, but I thought I'd save it for us.

I hung my new hottie clothes and put the sexy underthings in my drawers. When I was done, I already knew what I wanted to wear. It was a short, revealing clubbing dress with sheer thigh-high stockings and some strappy, really high-heeled stilettos. I didn't wear a bra with the dress, since I didn't need one.

By the time I was done dressing, I was hard as a rock again. I figured Joey and I could get some take-out, have a few drinks at home, and then have some hot sex.

Joey came in and sat on the bed. She started slipping on her stockings, and she smiled at me, saying, "I'm so glad you dressed so nicely tonight. See? Isn't this better than you in sweats and a tee-shirt and me in my bathrobe?"

I nodded. "I'll say. You never looked so hot. I've never felt so horny. We're going to have a ball tonight. Maybe you're a psychiatrist for a reason. I think you saved our marriage, honey. You seem excited to look your sexiest and best again, and I love that."

She smiled. "Yes, I am excited for our new life together." She slid the dress over her curves. She didn't wear a bra, either, and her nipples were as hard as mine, showing through her top. She slid into her strappy heels, which were as fetishy as mine were. She put her jewelry on and sprayed perfume over her body.

She came over to me, covered me with a peculiar yet sexy and feminine scent. It seemed to make me hornier still. "Pheromone perfume," she said. "Makes men *really* horny."

I laughed. "I'm horny enough as it is."

She nodded and took two necklaces out of her jewelry box. She came over to me and showed me. "Put this noose around your nipple and pull it tight enough to keep it hard and make it feel nice. Then wrap the chain around your neck and over the other side, back down to the other nipple and connect that one. It will make them more obvious and will lead the eye to them because of the way the chain disappears under the top. I'll put mine on too."

I took it from her and tightened the first noose. It felt great and really made the nipple protrude under the dress. I did the other one and looked in the mirror. I was a total slut, and so was my wife. I loved it. We were gonna have the best sex ever tonight.

Joey came over to me and wrapped her arms around my shoulders. She kissed me deeply on my lips and rubbed my crotch with her hand. "Mmm," she said. "You're so hot."

"You are too, sweetie. I love this."

"Good, girl. Sit on the bed for me."

I did, and she came over and knelt before me. She lifted my dress and slid the panties under my hairless balls and rod. She looked up to me as she grabbed it and wrapped her lips around it. She'd never sucked me after we were married. She bobbed her head twice on it, and I came instantly.

She stood and kissed me, shoving all of my semen into my mouth. I swallowed it. *Not a big deal*, I thought. It was worth it having her give me a BJ. The rest of the night would be incredible if this was any indication.

She said, "Fast as usual. I didn't think that would take long. Good girl. We're not wasting too much time. Did your come taste okay?"

"I guess. It wasn't as bad as I expected it to taste. Wasting time? What's the hurry?"

She went to the dresser, grabbed something from the drawer, and came back to where I sat on the bed, tucking my deflated thing away in my panties.

She knelt and grinned up at me. "Don't put it away yet. So your come tasted okay, huh? That's good. From that one taste I just had, I think yours is a little sweeter than most."

Sweeter than most? She was kneeling there, looking up at me and holding it between her thumb and forefinger. I thought, *Wow. Is she gonna do it again? From soft?*

She took a chrome ring and slid it over my limp rod, then stuffed my balls, one at a time, through it. I thought, *Cool, she's gotten some kinky toys for me too.*

Next she slid a tiny chrome hood with a hole in the tip over it and slid it all the way onto a peg on the ring. She threaded a lock through a hole and snapped it shut. It was now locked in some sort of tiny chrome cage.

She stood up. "Okay, now pull up your panties and let's go. To answer your question, why hurry, it's because we have a girls' night out tonight, and there are a ton of gorgeous hunks who are gonna be clubbing at the best pickup joint in the city. We're going out, girl! Woo hoo!"

"Wait, stop. I thought we were going to stay home and have dinner drinks and sex together."

She ginned a sideways grin. "Do you think you can have any sex in your new cage? I don't think so, Candy. Depending on how good you are tonight will determine when I take that thing off. Jerk a guy tonight, maybe. Suck a guy, hmm, probably. Let a guy fill your bottom, bingo! You're a winner and probably won't even *need* to take it off."

"Let's go."

5

What choice did I have if I ever wanted to come again? And in that body, and as horny as I was, that would be sheer torture. I had to do as she asked, or die.

I crossed and slid my sexy legs one over the other in the car as Joey drove; I filled my cage in my panties from the sensuality. I thought about what she said. Jerk a guy off, maybe. Suck, probably, and fill my bottom was the bingo prize, and I could get the cage off and come.

Well, I wasn't letting any guy win bingo in my bottom. Sounded gross and probably painful as hell. Not to mention degrading, being used as a sex object. None of it sounded at all cool, but I had to do something or risk having nothing myself.

Or maybe I'd just refuse to do anything, screw what she said, and just live in this cage and give up sex altogether. I could join a nunnery or something. But I still had a dick. Well, maybe I could be a priest. Yeah right, Candy, the slutty-looking priest. And neither option would solve my horniness. Shit!

We walked into the club, our fetishy heels making for short strides, clicking on the tile, my apple bottom swaying with each step, and my breasts bouncing with their hard nipples. We were like sex-object bookends, judging by the way all the guys—and even the girls—stared at us.

Joey held her head high as she strutted though the place. We were leaving a wake of gawkers behind us as she led me by the hand into the VIP room in the back. Evidently this room was where the rich guys had their fun at the club.

Bottles, mixers, and glasses were lined up on the bar, and there was no bartender. I went straight to it and poured myself two fingers of bourbon and slugged it down. Damn, I needed that.

Joey grabbed my hand on the bottle as I went to pour the next one. "Girls don't drink bourbon. Have a vodka instead."

I grabbed the Grey Goose and poured a shot. I turned around to lean against the bar and sip it. Joey poured herself one and leaned back with me. "See? This place is hoppin'. And aren't these guys hunks? I mean, there isn't a single one who's as wimpy as you were."

The music outside in the club thumped a rhythm of sex. There were some other girls in the room, but none as hot or good-looking as us, and certainly none with eraser-like nipples poking out of their dresses.

Some of the girls were sitting on the couches, leaning into the guys they were with, rubbing their crotches or kissing them. It looked aboveboard enough. Kinda like a lobby of a brothel. I doubted anyone would have sex there or do any more than they were doing now.

I thought I should be safe. Didn't want to be kissing a guy, though. As one girl was rubbing a guy's crotch, I wondered if doing that and making him come would count for my points. I could probably do that. I wouldn't really be touching it.

A couple of guys came over to us. "Hey, girls. You both look incredible. May we join you?"

Joey smiled. "Absolutely, boys. Thanks for the compliments. This is Candy, and I'm Joey."

They said their names, and I said a bimbo 'hi' and shook their hands.

The tall, handsome blond one named Keith said to me, "Candy is your name? Really? Did you change it?"

My bimbo voice came out as he watched me. "No, Candy's my name. My mom loved candy." I laughed, and a bimbo laugh came out.

"I see." He chuckled and slid alongside me at the bar. "Maybe we should take a seat on one of the couches."

I looked at Joey. She nodded and tugged the hand of her tall, dark, and handsome one named Derek, and we all carried our drinks to the couch. I sat on the cool leather seat, tugging my dress down with one hand, tucking it under my thighs. I crossed my legs and bounced a high heel nervously.

Derek wasted no time with Joey, who was sucking his face and rubbing his crotch. I looked at Keith and smiled, not knowing what to do. He seemed familiar in some way.

He said, "You look nervous, Candy. Is something wrong?" He ran his hand gently over my hair. "You're so pretty, and I feel I already know you well."

"You do? How, Keith?"

"I know we just started talking, but I think I really know the you inside." His gaze covered my body, examining each inch of me. "You seem to be so at home in your skin. Such a perfect fit of the soul to the body."

That was quite the compliment from someone I didn't know. His eyes ended up on mine as he placed a strong hand on my stockinged thigh and floated it up and down. It felt so good! I placed my hand on his and pressed it tightly to my leg so he'd keep doing it.

"Does that feel nice, Candy? It feels *very* nice to me."

"Oh yes, Keith. It feels wonderful. Please, don't stop."

I was hard in my cage form the sensuality of his hand on me. Weird that I should be turned on by a guy like that, but I think it was the stockings and the silkiness. What should I do now? I looked around the room.

Someone went to the door and locked it. They rang a bell next to it. Girls started unzipping pants, and some of them lifted their dresses and guided their men into them. Legs wrapped around the guys as they penetrated the girls—against the bar and on the couches —and the whole room turned into a sex party.

Joey was sitting on Derek's lap, facing him and lifting herself while she guided his thick, hard pole into her. She lowered herself onto it slowly, her eyes wide, looking into his eyes until she was impaled on it. "Oh baby," she said to him. "Mmm, nice."

My wife was getting laid by some other guy and loving every second. I'd never seen her so into it. I was jealous as hell, and my heart raced in my chest, yet it was the best porn ever.

"You okay, Candy?" Keith asked as he slid back on the couch, lifted my legs onto his lap, turning me onto the loveseat. I leaned against the armrest, and I kept my legs crossed, lest he learn my secret. He massaged my thighs as he smiled at me and lifted his hips against my legs, pressing his hardness, still in his pants, against them. It was rigid as a log.

"Is this all right, Candy?"

"Love the massage Keith. Is it okay for you? I'm not crushing you, am I?"

"Oh no. Not at all. You're as light as a feather. Your legs are so sexy and feel so smooth in the stockings. Would it be okay if I undid my zipper?"

"I guess. Go ahead and enjoy my legs. I love that you love them."

He slid his hands under my legs, undid his zipper and opened his trousers, pulling out a cleanly shaved package with a huge pole that he slid between my legs. He pumped it up and out of them, making it look like a gopher coming out of a hole and retreating.

It looked kind of silly, but it felt rather nice, and it was actually quite flattering to think I was exciting him so much. But heck, I excited myself, so why not other guys? Still, to have another person so enthralled with me was very gratifying.

I watched it as if it were a toy going in and out of my legs and not real. It was firm and thick with smooth, velvety, pinkish skin, and the head, large and purplish, oozed a glistening drop from the tip. It was much more pleasant to look at than I could have imagined. Was my brain changing like my body had?

I couldn't resist the urge to touch it. I wrapped my long-nailed fingers around it when it came up between my stockinged legs and let it slide into my loose fist. It was velvety smooth and warm. I squeezed it for a moment when it next poked though. It titillated me how was exquisitely firm it was, sending a chill through me and making me want to break free from my cage.

"That feels fantastic, Candy. Thank you," he said.

"It *is* nice, Keith. You're so large and hard, but the skin is so velvety. It actually looks beautiful to me. I love it."

He started to hump it up into my legs and hand more passionately. He smiled. "So glad you like it so much. Mmm, I think I have to finish like this if that's okay."

I wanted to see him release his passion over me. I wanted him to be that enraptured with me. "Oh god, yes, Keith. Please, *please* do.

He gazed adoringly at me. "It feels so good, and I love looking at all of you. You're like a goddess in front of me. Would you rub your breast for me?"

I took one hand and massaged it and squeezed my nipple. It made me want more. My cage was filled rock solid, and it wouldn't grow any further. It was pure torture.

Keith said, "You have gorgeous breasts. Can I suck your nipple while I do this?"

No one would blink an eye here, so I slid one out and sat closer to him so he could reach it. He sucked it in its noose, and my head rolled back on my shoulders with the pleasure it gave me. It was gliding lustfully in my one hand as he sped up the pace and had sex with my stockinged legs and hand.

He moaned around my nipple, nibbling and sucking, as I supported his head so he wouldn't stop delighting my breast. He sent luscious ripples through me. He pulled his head off and looked into my eyes with a bit of regret. "God, Candy, I'm gonna come on your leg... all right?"

I stroked his head affectionately. "God yes. *Please!*" I offered my breast, and he sucked and squeezed it as he lunged into my legs and hand. "Ungh god!" he mumbled around my nipple.

Warm sticky wetness shot into the air and onto my sheer black stockings, my hair, and my dress. Loads and loads of it, in long white strings, one after the other. It seemed it would never end.

But to my woe, it did end. It throbbed a couple more times in my fist, white cream dripping down the head. I gave it a goodbye kiss on the tip before he managed to slip it free. I swung my legs down and crossed them, moving close to him on the loveseat and wrapping my hands around his bicep. He tucked things away. I wished it had lasted longer because I was still horny as hell, and that had only made me hornier.

I started to wipe his come off me with a tissue. He grabbed my hand. "No, stop, let it stay. I like seeing it on you. You look even more seductive that way."

I stopped. Heck, why not? I could feel some dripping down my cheek.

"See, it looks so nice dripping on you like that. Very sexy."

Some dripped down to my lips. I licked it off. "If you say so. Thanks."

I know the old me would have loved seeing a girl with my finish on her. There was something erotic about it.

Keith began to massage my legs, his deposited wetness spreading over them like expensive skin cream. I sipped my drink and looked around, enjoying the worship he was giving me. Joey's guy was coming inside her as I sipped. "Ungh god, yeah! Fill me, baby."

I could see his come oozing out around out of her as he came, grunting and shoving up into her. I'd never seen her feel so good. Maybe she was right to do what she did to me. I deserved it, and she deserved more than I could give.

A kiss landed on my cheek. "You okay, Candy?" Keith asked.

I nodded and smiled.

"I'll be ready in a few minutes, and if you want, I can try to make you feel as good as your friend Joey does now."

I relished his leg massage and looked into his pleading eyes. He was so handsome and cute. He truly seemed caring and sincere, and I even felt a warm familiarity with him.

Then he said, "Or not. That is, if you'd rather not, since we just met. I don't want to push you into anything."

"Thanks. We'll see. I'm a little different from Joey, you know. Uh, I'm not as much of a woman as she is."

"Oh Candy, you're all woman. You're more woman than you know. I'm in love with you like I've always been that way."

He kissed me deeply while squeezing my breast and massaging my leg. God, it felt good being wanted and loved. Keith was so great. I felt like I've always loved him too.

6

Keith refilled our drinks while I watched Joey and Derek snuggle and chat quietly, his arm around her, her hand on his lap.

"Here ya go, my sweet, Candy." He smiled as he handed me my martini, then sat next to me. His slid his arm around me. "Is this okay?"

Actually, it felt terrific to me. I felt very protected and safe as well as loved. "Yes, I like that." I drank down half the martini and was finally ready to relax. "I like you, Keith. You seem like a nice guy."

"Thanks."

We chatted about his life, and he was intelligent, charming, flattering and successful, on top of his good looks, and he made me feel better than any woman *ever* had. We had another drink, and close to the end of that one, I was feeling pretty good about myself and the new me.

I looked over to Joey and Derek, and she had unzipped his pants. She took it all out and held his it, then took all of it into her mouth and sucked, bobbing her head on it, trying to get it hard. Her eyes smiled up at me and rolled in their sockets; she motioned with one hand for me to do the same to Keith.

She had said if I sucked a guy, I could probably come later that night, and I desperately needed to come. I bet Keith would love it if I did that for him.

Keith saw me watching them. He whispered in my ear, "That looks nice. Joey seems to like Derek as much as I like you. She's trying to get him hard again with her mouth. Ever do that? Get a guy hard with your mouth?"

"Uh, I..." I looked at his pants. He moved my hand to his zipper. "You can try it if you want."

I don't know if it was the buzz from the booze that forced me to do it, but I felt alive and good about it as I unzipped his pants and took him out. It wasn't completely shrunken, but it was much smaller and bent (even though it was still larger than mine when it was hard).

I leaned down and took it into my mouth, his cologne filling my nostrils with a luscious scent. It felt as silky and smooth as it had in my hand but even better in my mouth. Who knew sucking a guy could be so good?

I sucked it gently and slid my lips on it while running my tongue around it. I tugged his balls gently. It began to grow in my mouth. I became exhilarated, knowing it was working. I anxiously sped up my pace, my actions making his rod fill my mouth, and it kept growing until I had to use both a hand and my mouth to pamper all of it properly.

He placed his hands gently on my head and said, "Candy, that's wonderful. I love what you're doing to me. Don't stop making me feel this nice. Not ever."

My heart raced from the thrill of realizing how good it felt to have someone else love what I was doing to them. I looked up into his beautiful, loving eyes as he filled my mouth with his magic wand of passion and his energy for me.

He began to lift his hips in time with me and made it go as deep as I would let it. My other hand wrapped around the firm, warm shaft, limiting the depth of his penetration. My own swollen meat was trying to break open the cage that entrapped it.

I savored every second of sucking him and looking into his eyes, which expressed how deeply he was loving my ministrations. He petted my head and touched my cheek with the back of his fingers as he gazed affectionately at me, while it went in and out of my mouth. He said softly, "You're so beautiful to watch when you're doing that."

He squeezed my head tightly with both hands. "Oh, Candy, god." He thrusted gently into my face. "This is it, baby. If you don't want to swallow, you'd better let go."

I gripped his shaft tightly with my hand and tugged on his balls as he grunted and shoved into my face, his eyes on mine, his face contorting. "Ungh, god, yes." He shuddered. I was filled with his enamoredness for me, and my heart was full of love for it.

The first flood swelled through my fist and into my mouth. I swallowed in a panic as he pummeled my face and shot load after load into me. I slipped off it at one point and received a load onto my hair, but I hurriedly got back on it for the rest of the wonderful compliment he was paying me.

When he finished, I couldn't stop myself and kept trying to get more from him. His body jerked, and he struggled to get my head away from him. "Stop. Candy, please..." I raced my tongue around the head of it. He shuddered. "Stop." He tugged my head off him.

I sat up licking my lips, smiling at him.

He said, "Wow, are you good! You were so enthusiastic about that. I loved it."

"Thanks. I loved it too. I've never been so engaged in something." I felt my face flush. I had enjoyed that better than any sex I'd ever had. I knew I was hooked.

He zipped up and stood. "I have to go. I have workers coming over to the house early in the morning to refurbish some things, and I have to be there. May I see you again?"

I nodded. He leaned down and kissed me on the lips. "Good. Have a good night, Candy."

I watched him leave. How would he contact me? I had to see him again.

I stood, went to the bar and got a drink that I didn't really need with the buzz I had already. I sat back down on the couch next to Derek and Joey. Joey was wiping her lips. She smiled at me. She leaned over and whispered, "Yours is sweeter, dear. How was Keith's? I'm proud of you. You *might* have to get a reward tonight."

"Thanks. I'm proud of me, too, and do I ever need that reward! I think the cage is going to break. Keith was awesome. I hate to hear myself say it, but I loved every second."

"Good. Now you need to meet some of the other available boys before we go. I want you to chat with them and suck some more so you can compare. If you do that. I'll be sure you come tonight, baby."

Coming sounded great, but I didn't know if I'd last that long anyway. "Joey, I'm kind of spent. This was so much for one night."

"I know, but I want you to see how other guys are too. Then you'll see if Keith is still special to you or not. Take this."

She dug in her purse and took out a pill. "It will help you feel more energetic." She handed it to me.

I looked at it.

She said, "It's like a five-hour energy drink but in a pill. You'll see—you'll feel energized again. It's safe."

I downed the pill. She leaned back and chatted with Derek. I looked around the room. In a few minutes, my energy was up, and I decided I had to do what she said. Not just for her, but for me as well.

7

I went to the bar and chatted with some of the guys. They were okay, but didn't seem as nice as Keith. I decided rather than waste my time with them, I'd just use them and indulge my curiosity, seeing if it was as good with them as it had been with Keith.

I looked at all of them. "Okay, guys. I'm getting hungry, and I need some protein." I put my drink on the bar and knelt on a pillow on the floor, looking up at them. I reached my arms out and licked my lips.

They all lined up, surrounding me, and unzipped, taking my treats out for me. There were three of them in front of my face. I grabbed one and slipped it into my mouth and grabbed two others with my hands and jerked them.

They weren't as long or thick as Keith's but were equally silky in my hands and mouth. I immersed myself in the men's excitement for me—I longed to make them come. I worked my way around the circle of firm-fleshed pacifiers.

The first one, whom I'd had in my mouth, was now jerking it as he watched me. He shoved the guy in my mouth aside and slipped his between my lips, grabbing my head tight.

He said, "That's it, you little bimbo slut. Suck me and make me come." He squeezed my head with his big hands and humped into my mouth hard, almost gagging me, and then he came, flooding my mouth. He pulled out and jerked the rest all over my hair and face.

The next one slapped my face with his dick repeatedly while he called me whore and slut and bitch, then he stuffed it in my mouth and came while I greedily swallowed it all. The third came, wrapping my hair around it and pumping into it, making my scalp all wet and soaking my hair.

When he was done, three more took their places. Only the last one treated me kindly. He coddled my head and gently thrusted into my mouth, looking into my eyes, making me want to make him feel good. I became passionate about sucking his, and wanted him to experience how good I could be, rather than just being a lustful receptacle like I was for the last ones.

I accomplished my goal with him, and when he was done, he helped me stand. He took me away from the others waiting to use me. We sat on a couch.

He said, "You don't have to do every guy, honey. You can stop whenever you want. I thought it looked like things were getting rough for you. You're so hot—every guy wants you."

"Thanks. I guess I just got carried away." I looked down at my dress, my chest covered in random splats of white drips. "Wow. I guess I really did get carried away. Thanks."

Joey stood before us. "Ready to go home, Candy? Seems you had a good time tonight." She looked at the guy sitting with me. "Thanks, Bill, for saving her. I saw she was getting too frenzied, and the guys were, too, and they were treating her rudely. It was nice of you to help her."

"No problem, Joey. He stood and kissed her on the lips. He looked down at me. "Thanks, Candy. Have a great night. Get some rest."

"Thanks, Bill."

Joey took me by the hand and I stood with her. "Let's go home, Joey."

"Exactly. Time for your reward, Candy."

8

There was no reward. We got home, and I fell into bed as soon as we got there. I woke in the morning trying to comb my semen-glued hair loose. I washed my face and wiped off my dress with a wet washcloth as well as I could. Somehow, all of that didn't disgust me in the least, but rather, it gave me proud memories of how I'd obtained it. In mincing steps in my fetishy heels, I paraded into the kitchen, where Joey was cooking breakfast.

Standing in her sweats, cooking bacon, she beamed at me. "Hi, Candy! My, you were *something* last night. For someone who didn't want to do what you did, you sure got into it. Seems you've become the talk of the club."

I sat at the table and looked down at it. "Yeah, I was *crazed* with desire. It was illuminating."

She sat next to me. "That's good, honey. Now maybe you'll see how wonderful it would be to have a real man to please all the time. In other ways too—a man who will make hot and heavy love to you. I think you'll love it."

I shook my head. "No. Not that. Never."

"You loved making Keith feel good in two different ways. Why do you think him making love to you would be bad?"

"I don't know. It just would. I can't imagine having something stuffed into me down there, no matter how good it feels for him. I mean, have you ever heard of anyone saying they can't wait to go see their proctologist? I just want to eat, shower, and relax. Maybe watch some ESPN. Hang out in sweats."

"Okay, honey."

We ate in silence, and I showered and cleaned out like Joey said girls did. I did my hair and felt refreshed. The only problem was that the shower made me aware of how sexy my body was, and it made me horny and hard in the cage again.

I slid on some sweats and then immediately slipped them off. They didn't feel right. I dressed in a short mini sundress with stockings and heels, and my body was sensual, tingling, and alive. I clip-clopped my way into the great room.

Joey looked at me. "What? No sweats?"

"Uh, they didn't feel as nice. They felt sloppy and ugly."

"I see. I have ESPN on. There's soccer and football today."

I sat on the couch. "Uh, what I really need is to collect my reward from last night so I *can* relax. Please, take this cage off?"

She smirked. "Uh, I don't know, young lady. With the attitude you have toward furthering your experience and indulging in the pleasures of making love with a man, I think you should stay in the cage until you're ready to be a big girl."

I crossed my legs and looked at the TV. I bounced one foot over the other. I was hard in the cage, and I felt like a nymphomaniac. This couldn't work.

I turned to Joey and gave her my best doe eyes and whimpered, "Please, please, Joey, please let me take the cage off and come. Then I can relax a little, and maybe then I'll think about it more. Right now I just need to release the pressure."

She stared at me thinking. "Okay, under one circumstance."

"Anything. Anything, I promise."

"Okay. Remember you said that, young lady."

She went and brought the key back. She wagged it in front of my face, one hand behind her back. "Now get on the floor on all fours."

I hurriedly did so, looking up at her.

She said, "Now lean down and put your forearms on the floor and rest your face on them."

I did, trying to see her, but she went behind me. She lifted my dress onto my back. She slid my panties down. The cool air hit my butt cheeks. I felt a cool wetness drip between my cheeks. Something slid between them, and it found my hole and was pressed against it. "Hey, Joey, stop."

"Now relax."

I tried to relax. Just the thought of her putting something into me was making me nervous.

She massaged my back with one hand while pressing a little harder each time at my hole. It went deeper each time, stretching me a little more, and then it slid in, and my hole clenched around it. A vibration started. She slid my panties back up.

"Okay, sweetie, you can get up."

I stood, and the sensations it created made me even harder and hornier. I sat on the couch. I wriggled my butt against it.

She watched me. "Feels nice, doesn't it?"

"Nice yeah, surprisingly nice...too nice. It's making me hornier."

"See, having something in there isn't so bad at all, is it?"

"I guess not, if it's a special toy like that."

She tossed me the key. "Okay, dear, whack that monkey, and we can watch sports like you wanted to."

I nervously undid the cage, took it off, and stood in my heels. It throbbed in the air beneath my dress. I wrapped my silky dress around it and slid the fabric against it, and it shot immediately. I whimpered, my eyes closed, "Huh, uh, god, huh..." Load after heavy load shot from me into the fabric as my body shook and shuddered. The vibrator inside me seemed to make it more intense than it had ever been before.

My knees went weak, and I slumped onto the couch, rested my head back, and caught my breath. Joey slid over and snuggled up, peppering my cheeks with kisses. "My lovely girl. Was that nice? Didn't the thing in your bottom make it feel better than ever?"

Catching my breath, I opened my eyes and placed my hand on her hair and stroked it. "It was lovely. Very nice. Thank you for that."

"Good girl. I'd say you're now ready for a deflowering."

"What? No way. I don't want a guy in there. Never."

She sat up and smirked at me. "We'll see about that." She took the cage in her hands.

"Joey, no, please!"

She put it back on me and locked it. "You just tell me when you're ready, and you won't have to wear it anymore. Go put on some clean clothes and we can watch TV."

9

It was such a relief having the monkey off my back. I put the dress in the hamper and slipped on a cozy sweater dress. I went back out and sat next to Joey. She snuggled next to me, wrapping her hands around my bicep. "You make such a lovely girl, honey. I love you this way."

"Thanks, Joey. I feel much better—now I can relax and enjoy just being with you and the new me and some ESPN. Can I take out this plug?"

"Not yet, honey. Let it stay in there. Is it bothering you?"

"Well, it does feel good, but soon I'll have another monkey on my back, and I have enough stimulation with this body alone."

"As long as it's not hurting you, you're wearing it. Now relax and enjoy some TV. I'll make us some popcorn."

We ate popcorn and watched tennis for a while. I felt wonderfully feminine and nice for those few minutes. Then the monkey started to return, and soon my cage was filled. I was back to being my horny self.

"Shall we go to the club?" Joey asked when dinnertime was approaching. "We could get a nice meal and then go out."

"Uh, I'd rather not get all crazed again. Do you think I'll ever see Keith again? He said he'd like to."

"You could bump into him at the club. But I'm sure he'll be calling you. I gave him your number already, and he has mine."

"Good." I wondered when she could have given it to him last night. I didn't remember her having the opportunity. Oh well, I must have missed it. "I'd rather wait until he calls than go crazy at the club again. It was a little embarrassing, even though I enjoyed it."

"I told him not to call you until you were ready."

"Why? We don't have to do that. I could still make him happy and be with him."

"That's not fair to him. When you're ready, let me know, and I'll let him know, and we can set something up for your defloration and get on with our lives as they should be."

The vibrator hummed inside me, and I was as horny as ever. I wondered what was actually holding me back from doing it. I guessed it was my old paradigms of identity, because of what I have between my legs. I looked at Joey observing me as I thought.

I took a deep breath. "I'm not ready. I don't know why."

"Take your time, dear. If you want to stay home, I'll give Derek a call, and he can entertain us tonight if you like."

"So you knew Derek before last night?"

"Uh, yeah, we've been enjoying each other for years. He's made love to me many more times than you have."

"Really?"

"Really."

I didn't know what to think. But what did it matter now anyway? Joey and I had never had a normal guy-girl relationship, really. I saw how happy he made her last night, and it was something I never could have done. It wasn't like she was leaving me for him.

I nodded. "I see. I don't blame you. I understand. I never saw you as fulfilled as you were last night."

She snuggled and kissed my cheek. "It doesn't mean I don't love you, because I wouldn't be going through all this if I didn't. I'd just leave you."

"I understand. It's all good. If you want to invite Derek over, you can. I mean, I guess you don't need my permission, but if you feel like it, we can do that."

"You know what? I'd rather just stay home and cuddle with you."

She kissed my lips deeply and caressed my stockinged thigh. I wanted to make love to her.

I asked her, "Honey? Can I make love to you?"

"Oh, sweetie, Derek made me sore last night. I'm sorry. Besides, you're a beautiful girl now and deserve to be treated like one."

We watched more TV, my cage filled, my body alive as Joey continued to caress me—sliding her hand on my legs, squeezing my breasts, sucking my nipples and nibbling them. Oh, god.

10

We spent day after day just enjoying each other, Joey loving and caressing me. I was at my wits' end. It was wonderful, but the monkey was growing into a full-grown gorilla. At the end of a wonderful evening, after a romantic dinner on the town together, we came home and changed into our sexy, seductive nightclothes. Joey was dressing and looking better than ever, and so was I.

We sipped wine on the couch. "Joey, don't you want to have Derek? I mean, it's been days."

"Of course I do. But you're holding things up. I want you to have Keith first. Then we can see how our lives will be structured."

"Our lives? Why would they be any different?"

"Well, once you fulfill your final experience, you might want to live with a man as well."

"I'd never want to leave you."

"I know. I wouldn't want to leave you either. But Keith may want to be without you."

I took a deep breath. "Yes, it would become more complicated, possibly, but you deserve to be with Derek."

Joey leaned in, her face pleading. "It *could* be that way. We could all be together. All of us. Why not?"

"Well, first off, Keith doesn't know I'm not really a woman down there. When he finds out, he might just want to beat me to death."

"Do you think he's like that?"

"No, but you never know."

"Keith has a girl like you at his house. She cooks and cleans for him and lives there."

"He does?"

"Yes."

"Well that doesn't mean he'd want a person like that as a girlfriend."

"Honey, he knows what you are, and he wants you. He's always wanted you all those years since he left."

"He's always...? What?"

"Yes, you two went to school together. He moved away in eighth grade."

I put my hand over my mouth. I was dumbfounded. "Oh my god! That's the same Keith? We used to be the best of friends. We even did things that two boys shouldn't have. After he was gone, I vowed *never* to do such things again, and I didn't. As I grew up, I reflected upon it as if it were just a stupid part of being a kid."

"Yes, honey. Same Keith. He did the same thing after he left and never allowed himself to enter that territory again. Then he reached out to find you, and he found we were together on social media, so he contacted me."

"Wow. So, you made me into this *for him*?"

"Him, you, me...all of us, I guess. He truly loves you. He always has and hasn't been able to stop thinking about you. But that has always been forbidden fruit for him, to even think about being with a male. He couldn't do it. He was afraid of talk. It happens, even in this day and age of coming out and openness."

I was full of thought. He was my best friend, and I had never even tried to find him for fear we'd go back to what we did as kids. I remembered him saying that night at the club how familiar I was to him. How he loved me. How beautiful I was. He remembered me. That's why I fell for him so quickly. I remembered him subconsciously and fell in love so fast. I had always loved him.

"This is wonderful, Joey. I can hardly believe it. I can't believe you would do this for me. I love you so much." I hugged her to me and kissed her hair. "Mmm."

My heart raced in my chest. Joey was patiently waiting for me to think this through while she caressed my stockinged legs and gazed lovingly into my eyes.

I pulled back and looked at her. "It could work. If we had a bigger place, we could figure it all out. I'd love to have Keith around."

I stood up and beamed down at her. My heart said this was perfect. "Okay, let's set up my, uh, deflowering, honey. I can't hold our lives back any longer. You need Derek. I want Keith. And most of all, I want you to be happy. I need to step up to being who I am now."

Her eyes flew open, her mouth went wide, her hand covered her mouth. "Oh, my god! Thank you, Candy. You'll be so glad you did."

She tossed me the keys to the cage and took out her phone. She looked at me while it rang. "You can go take the cage off and the plug out now, too, if you like. You're gonna be a big girl soon and don't need any more training."

11

Joey told Keith I was ready, and we were invited over to for a fabulous dinner prepared by his cook and housekeeper. It was to be the night he would make love to me for the first time. My deflowering was to happen.

I was quite nervous and wanted everything to be right. Joey and I had gone shopping for new outfits for the evening; I wanted to feel as feminine and pretty as possible. I bought a lovely, short, V-neck dress. The dress itself was a thin, almost sheer, light pink satiny fabric, and the top held my breasts firmly, creating gorgeous cleavage and revealing my eraser-like nipples through it.

The skirt was lined with several layers of soft crinoline, which caressed my thighs when I walked, flared the skirt out, and looked fluffy and feminine. I wore white ruffled, lacy, crotchless panties, which allowed my little guy to stand up freely and lifted the whole package so it could be caressed by the soft crinoline as I walked. God it felt *sooo* good and *sooo* feminine!

I wore sheer white gartered stockings, a white lace garter belt, strappy, fetishy, high-heeled white shoes that forced me to take tiny steps and made me feel vulnerable. I looked sinfully seductive and feminine as I walked in mincing steps, my breasts heaving and bouncing with each step. I looked, and felt, like I needed a good pounding and I couldn't wait for it from Keith.

Joey wore a much simpler outfit. It was a short, tight, revealing black dress with only black stockings and a garter belt with crotchless panties and heels as high as mine.

Her nipples were like headlights as she beamed at me, observing me as I checked myself in the full length mirror. "You look incredible, honey. How does that dress feel? It looks so feminine and almost sissy-like."

"I love it. It makes me feel like I want to be submissive and taken by a real man." I turned to face her. "And you, my sweet, look like you're ready to get laid. All he has to do is lift the hem and slip it in. I can't wait to see you with Derek." I kissed her lightly on the lips.

Her hand tried to find my little guy through the layers of crinoline. "Gosh, where is he hiding?"

"He's there in a soft little nest of crinoline."

I moved her hand to it and she wrapped her hand around it. "Mmm, very nice. You're ready."

"I am. Let's get this show on the road. I can't wait any longer."

We drove to Keith's house, which was in an upscale suburb, out of town a ways. We entered the gates and climbed the switchback driveway to the circle in front. The car rumbled across the pavers until we parked in front of the granite steps.

We climbed them carefully, hand in hand. Joey said, "Isn't it gorgeous? Do you think there will be room for all four of us to live here?"

"Oh, my god, Joey. I never would have imagined."

"Yes, Keith has been a big success."

The doorbell clanged a deep slow tune that we heard through the door. One of the huge double doors opened to reveal a pretty, smiling woman. "Hi Joey." She gave Joey a kiss on the cheek. "And this must be Candy. So pleased to meet you, honey. You turned out so lovely. I'm jealous." She laughed and kissed me on the cheek. "Please, come in. Keith and Derek are having drinks in the parlor."

She led us to them, walking before us. She wore a short French maid's outfit in black with white crinoline under the skirts. Her breasts bounced as she walked in tiny steps like ours, all our heels clattering on the marble. Her long blond hair swung from side to side over her hips, her wrists bent, as her arms added femininity to her seductive walk. I found it hard to believe she too had male parts under that dress.

"Gentlemen, the ladies have arrived," she announced to the men as they sat in a leather sofa conversation pit by the fire, sipping bourbons. They stood, flashing wide eyes and smiles at us. A smile filled my face ear to ear as I saw my best friend from years ago in a new light.

He came over to me and gave me a big hug. "Finally. Finally, we can be together and rekindle what we had so many years ago. Thank you for making this possible." He kissed me deeply on the lips. I seemed to melt in his arms.

"Oh, Keith, if I had known sooner, I might have done it all on my own to be with you."

"I didn't want you to have to make that choice. Joey and I came up with this plan so that if you didn't want to be with me again, at least you'd be who you were always meant to be." He peppered my face with tiny kisses. "I love you, Candy. Always have."

"I love you too, Keith."

"Hey, love birds," Derek said as he stood with his arm around Joey. "Like a drink, Candy? Yvette is waiting to take your order and she's a busy girl."

Yvette stood with her hands behind her back, smiling and waiting patiently. Her bright blue eyes, high cheek bones, and luscious lips made her look more of a model than a chef and maid.

I was taken with her and stood with my mouth open, just staring at her face.

She said, "Candy? Are you okay?"

"Uh, yeah. Sorry—you're just so stunning."

"Thank you. Drink?"

"Yes, please, Yvette. Goose martini, up, dirty, olives."

"Wonderful. I'll be right back with everybody's cocktails."

She turned, and I watched her until she turned the corner. I turned back to Keith. "Wow, she's something."

"She is a wonderful woman. She takes such good care of me and the house and anyone in it. You'll love her."

"I think I will. She's really like me?"

"Yes. I think you're even more beautiful."

"Thanks."

"Let's sit." He took me by the hand, and we sat on the couch opposite Derek and Joey, who were cuddled together with Derek's hand resting on Joey's crossed knee. They smiled up at us as we sat down together.

Joey said to me, "See? Isn't this nice?"

"It's wonderful. A dream come true." I turned to Keith. "So this is where we're all going to live?"

"If you choose to. Derek is moved in, and we'll move you and Joey in if you both want to. I know that's Joey's plan, at least. I guess it's up to you, dear."

I nodded excitedly and kissed his cheek. "Absolutely!"

Yvette placed our drinks in front of us. "Anything else before I finish making dinner?" She looked at all of us.

Keith said. "Yvette, appetizers? Uh, this *is* a special night, so if you're too busy or don't feel like it or just would rather not, you don't have to but—"

Her eyes popped open wide, and a smile filled her face. "Nonsense. I'd love to. You know how much pleasure it gives me to serve those appetizers." She laughed and ran off.

Keith caressed my stockinged legs. "You look so feminine and submissive tonight, Candy. I love it."

I placed my hand on his crotch to feel how hard he was, and he was throbbing for me, as I was for him, in my nest of crinoline. "Thank you. I wanted to feel like that and have a real man take me. I've been thinking about this all week."

I took his hand and placed it on my breast. We kissed and he squeezed my nipple through the thin fabric. I could have come right then if I wanted to, but I wanted to save it for the special moment when he took me.

Keith took a breast from my dress and began to suck my nipple. I leaned back to hold his head and enjoy his ministrations while I watched Derek with his hand under Joey's dress, his arm moving in and out, Joey holding his head while her head rolled on her shoulders.

I rubbed Keith's in his pants and wanted to suck it.

In came Yvette with a strap over her shoulders and around her waist. It was attached to a tray, which would remain stable should she let it go of it—like those cigarette girls in the old movies. The tray held silver bowls with different dips. She came over to me first. Keith sat up and put me back in my dress. I adjusted my breasts. "Sorry, Yvette."

"Oh don't mind that. It's perfectly fine here. We're all very open. Would you like some dip? I have lobster, clam, and a slightly spicy chili dip."

I looked at the tray. There were no crackers or veggies or anything to dip. I looked up at her. She said, "If you choose the chili dip, all I suggest is that you clean it all off well; if left on too long it may burn. For a little while, though, it feels very nice. The lobster and clam are very cooling to follow the chili, and the contrast is lovely."

I looked at Keith. He smiled and nodded.

I asked her, "So do I put my finger in it?"

"Oh my, no. Don't mess your pretty nails and get it all under them. Allow me when you're ready."

I thought, *Interesting. She's going to dip her finger in them and let us lick them off. How kinky.*

"Yes please, Yvette, let me taste the chili one first."

"My favorite!" She let the tray go and it hung below her hem. She pulled her hem up and tucked it under the belt of the tray. She was long and thick and sticking out of crotchless panties, and there was a tiny black lace bib over her shaved balls. She held her rod with her long-nailed hands and dipped it into the bowl, then wiped the chili dip around her thick, long, hard shaft.

I stared at it. She looked at me. "It's getting warm, honey. You have to lick it off, or it'll burn me. Are you okay? Should I wipe it off myself?"

I stared at it. It was gorgeous and getting red as it throbbed in her fingers. I dove onto it, running my tongue around it and licking it clean. She put her hand gently on my head. "That's nice. Now try a cool one?"

I pulled off her and she dipped just the tip into the lobster one. "Now just lick it off and with your tongue—run it around to clean off the chili."

I did.

"That a girl, Candy. Now you've got it. Thank you."

I savored it for a minute, and then she touched my head. "Some more, or should I move around the room?"

I popped off her with a slurp and looked up at her. "It's gorgeous and wonderful, but I don't want to hog it."

"Of course." She moved to Keith who delightedly indulged, doing chili then lobster, then chili then clam. On she went to Joey and then to Derek. All of us watched the others as they dined on Yvette's gorgeous dipper. When she was done serving each of us, she looked around the room. "Anyone want seconds, or shall I finish and make dinner?"

Keith looked around the room, and when no one said anything he called Yvette over with his hand. "You can finish now, honey. I know I'm usually the lucky one who gets the reward, but why not give it to Candy tonight? I'm sure she'd love the offering."

Yvette looked to me. I nodded and smiled. "Love to."

She came over and held it for me while I dove onto it and tugged her balls while she thrust into my face, holding my head tight.

"Oh yes, Candy. You're the best. I'm coming, sweetie. Huh, uh..."

I swallowed as best I could the voluminous amount of her sweet cream—shot after shot, as she thrust into my face. Some dripped down my chin, but I managed to retain most of it. She pulled out when she was done and tucked it back under her dress. "That was wonderful, Candy. Thank you."

"No, thank you," I said, smiling up at her.

She reached down and wiped my chin off with a napkin. "There, all better. Another round of drinks, anyone? Dinner will be half an hour." She looked around, and everyone ordered another, as did I. Keith waved her on.

She returned with our drinks and took the empty glasses while we lounged and enjoyed being with our partners. Derek and Joey were slowly seducing each other. Keith and I were catching up on what had happened since we were young and touching each other like lovers do.

I was thrilled with how this was turning out and couldn't wait to have Keith make love to me. We drank the next drink, and Yvette ushered us into the dining room. The spread was incredible. Duck, salmon, steaks, and all sorts of sides. It was a feast for a king.

Yvette served wine and placed open bottles at each end for us to share. When she was satisfied with everything, she slid under the table, and I could feel her hands under my dress. She lifted my dress, and took me into her lips. She bobbed her head on it and sucked. I looked at Keith and he smiled. "If that's too distracting, she can stop. I thought it would be nice to get one out of the way so we can all last longer later."

I smiled. "Oh no, it's not...huh..." I grabbed the edge of the table as Yvette flicked my tip while tugging on my balls and sucking, then ran her tongue in wild circles around it while bobbing her head on it. "Ungh, god..." I came hanging on to the table trying not to thrash about under it. Yvette was kind and released me quickly, covering me with the fluffy nest of crinoline again. She patted my leg and crawled away to Keith.

We passed the plates and enjoyed a wonderful meal while everyone enjoyed the ministrations of Yvette, including Joey, who had to stop eating momentarily when she came a few times. When Yvette was done with Derek, she slid back out from under the table, wiped her lips with a napkin, and smiled at us all. "Anything else?"

I said to her, "Aren't you going to eat with us? It doesn't seem right."

"I normally do, but I asked Keith if I could do this for all of you, since this is such a special occasion. Thankfully, he allowed me to give you all these gifts. I wouldn't know what else to give, so it made it easy for me. I ate while I cooked and after I get things cleaned up, I'll be joining everyone. I love what I do and the life I have. Don't feel sorry for me, Candy."

I nodded and sipped my wine, finished the meal, ate dessert and espresso.

Keith stood. "Well, I don't know if I can wait any longer, so I think, if it's okay with my Candy, I'd like to take her upstairs. If you'd all like to join us, we can see what life will be like for us all when we have the time to enjoy each other." He placed his hand on mine and looked around the table. Everyone stood.

Keith led me by the hand up the winding triple staircase to a room with a bed larger than any I'd ever seen before. The covers were pulled back to reveal red satin sheets; a fire burning in the fireplace, and the lights were soft and warm. Keith lifted me onto the bed and pushed me back, wrapping his legs around mine, kissing me. He slid down and sucked my nipples.

I watched as Joey slid onto the other side and moved back to the head of the bed, her arms out for Derek. Derek stood nearby, stripping off his clothes to reveal a firm, lean, strong frame with a huge, shaved, gorgeous impaler, standing up above tight, shaved balls. It looked like a toy, not a real one, but it was very real, the way it was lifting and dropping in the air.

She began by sucking him, using both hands. Keith slid from my breast and lifted my dress onto my stomach. He held my hard rod with his forefinger and thumb and sucked it gently. I touched his head. "Don't make me come, baby. I want to save it for when you do."

He went slowly, driving me wild watching him, and he made me long for him inside me even more. I looked around and saw lube on the nightstand. I put some on a finger, and with my other hand, I moved Keith aside. He slid off the bed and stripped off his clothes, revealing his hard body.

I lubed myself, watching him jerk it while he looked into my eyes. When I was ready, I held my arms out to him. He slid onto the bed and between my legs. He pressed it into my hole. It stretched me and stretched me until it drove past the entrance. I whispered in his ear, "Oh god, Keith. That feels wonderful, honey."

Deeper and deeper he pushed it, impaling me on it until it felt he touched my heart...literally and figuratively. I was deeply in love.

I looked over to see Derek pounding into Joey over and over and Joey squeezing his hard ass tight, urging him on. Her breath was choppy and her eyes wide as she gazed into my eyes and came on him. Her body spasmed and shuddered as he continued to pound her.

All the while, Keith was making slow, deliberate love to me while he moaned, looking in my eyes, holding my heels by my head. My little rod stood straight up, oozing a steady stream down it. My body was electrified, every tactile and sensory sensation amplified while I looked into my lover's eyes and felt his passion infusing me.

The bed was still shaking from Derek, and I looked over to see Joey coming again on him. Derek's body went tense as he shoved his long, fat meat deep into her and held it there while he grunted and came in her.

The sight drove me to grab Keith's ass and squeeze it while making him go faster and deeper. "Fill me with your magic wand, Keith! Do it! I love being Candy!"

Did he ever. He rammed into me and over, his eyes locked on mine. I could see by his grimace he was about to come. I begged him, "That's it, baby, give it to Candy."

I glanced down to see myself flailing about with each thrust and throwing off drops of semen. He pounded, and as he came, I came, too, shooting it all over my belly and dress as it flailed in circles while he filled me with his lovely wetness.

He slid so smoothly then—it was some slick tool to take me to heaven as he shoved it all the way in and held it there. "Oh god, Candy."

I stroked his hair, and then he collapsed onto me, staying inside me. We all lay there, resting.

Yvette came into the room and sat on the bed. She stroked my hair. I gazed into her eyes. She smiled down at me. "Is it good being Candy?"

I smiled. It's wonderful, Yvette....It's absolutely dream-come-true, in-a-fairy-tale-wonderful being Candy." I closed my eyes and let Yvette run her hands over my hair and kiss my cheeks while Keith lay on top of me, his breath warm in my ear, still deep inside me as he said, "I love you, Candy."

I never felt more alive, more human, more in my skin, and more satisfied and fulfilled in my life. My monkey was gone, and I was me. I loved being Candy.

If you enjoyed this book, it would be great if you could leave a review and tell a friend about it, or blog it out. Thanks!

Barb and Thom

For more of our books, both fiction and non-fiction, go to:

Amazon:

http://www.amazon.com/Barbara-Deloto/e/B00J21HWA4/

Don't forget our website, which has more links to things you might like, as well as other places to get our works.

http://www.ShapeShifterBook.com

Made in United States
Orlando, FL
22 January 2024

42763200R10032